MY CAT,

Herman Bernard Fred Tigger Dusty Geronimo Mike

MY CAT,

Herman Bernard Fred Tigger Dusty Geronimo Mike

AND OTHER ANIMAL STORIES
Compiled by the Editors
of
Highlights for Children

Compilation copyright © 1995 by Highlights for Children, Inc.
Contents copyright by Highlights for Children, Inc.
Published by Highlights for Children, Inc.
P.O. Box 18201
Columbus, Ohio 43218-0201
Printed in the United States of America

ISBN 0-87534-634-0

Highlights is a registered trademark of Highlights for Children, Inc.

CONTENTS

MY CAT,

Herman Bernard Fred Tigger Dusty Geronimo Mike

By Deborah Morris

And why, you may ask, does my cat have seven names? I gave him only one when I got him. That was right after Mom and I first moved to Kingsley. We didn't know anybody, and it was pretty lonely, so Mom gave me a cat. Anyway, I named him Herman—not after anyone, just after himself. It was the only name my Mom suggested that I thought had character. And my cat does have character.

He's not like the finicky cats on TV commercials. In fact, he's very good-natured. I play with him a lot; but he never gets mad or grumpy, even when I accidentally squeeze his tail too hard. He doesn't swing from the drapes, piddle on the floor, or drag in dead mice. Mom would have a fit if he did that. He loves to play hide-and-seek. Sometimes he'll climb under my bedspread and then walk all around my bed. He is like a moving lump.

But most of all Herman loves to visit people. I didn't know this at first. All I knew was that he liked to go outside and stay out for hours at a time, sometimes even overnight.

Then one day I got a note. Herman brought it to me, attached to his collar. It said, "What is this cat's name?" Well, of course, I wrote down "Herman." And when he went outside again, I put the note back on his collar.

Again he was on one of his extended journeys, "to London and back," as my Mom always said. When he finally returned, the note was a bit worn, but still attached to his collar. I took it off to show Mom, but when I looked at it I just about dropped my teeth. This is what it looked like:

What is this cat's name? Herman Bernard Fred Tigger Dusty Geronimo Mike

At first I just stared in wonder at Herman. I'd never met anyone with more than three names. And he had seven!

But wait a minute, I thought. This is MY cat. And I gave him only ONE name. Who did these other people think they were?

So I wrote another note:

This is my cat. His name is Herman. He belongs to Abigail Kaufman, 5609 Birch St.

The next day when Herman went out, I attached the note to his collar. Then I was bombarded with notes, like this one: *Bernard visits Ted Johnson, 5611 Birch St.* And this one: *Tigger comes to see Joey Martin at 5620 Birch St.*

Everybody on the block sent me a note, saying that Herman (or Fred, or Dusty, etc.) came to visit them. Finally I got a note from the old lady who lives right next door to us. She wrote:

Dear Abigail,

I know that Mike (Herman) is your cat, but I hope you don't mind if he stops by to see me once in a while. He is very well mannered and doesn't scratch or beg for food, although he does enjoy a bowl of milk when I offer it to him. He often gets in my lap and goes to sleep as I stroke him. He's such good company, even though he stays only a little while. You're a very lucky girl to have a cat like Mike.

> *Yours truly,*
> *Mrs. Gregor*
> *5607 Birch St.*

All the notes, especially Mrs. Gregor's, made me feel bad. I had wanted Herman all to myself. Now I was ashamed. But what could I do?

Well, I decided to do what Herman did. I went visiting. I followed Herman, and I met every person on my block. Now I don't mind when Herman is gone for a long time, because I know where he is. He's visiting our friends.

In Search of Harvey

By Jeffie Ross Gordon

Harvey was missing! This was a job for Charles Worthington, Frog Finder.

"Charlie, you find that frog before your father comes home—or else," called mom from the kitchen.

"I'm trying to, Mom." I had to shout to be heard over the whirr of her food processor.

"I won't have Harvey disrupting our dinner by hopping across the dining room—again!"

Poor Harvey. He couldn't help it if he was an adventurous frog. Before he was my frog, he lived with Grandpa Worthington. But Grandpa got tired of looking for Harvey. He was always escaping from his tank—Harvey, not Grandpa—and hopping away, mostly at dinnertime. One day Grandpa sent Harvey to live with me. I was glad to adopt Harvey. My mother and father weren't so happy, especially when Harvey got adventurous. One of these days, I was afraid my mother would follow through on her "or else."

"Harvey, where are you?" I slithered along the living room carpet and lifted the ruffled skirt of the couch, then peered into the darkness. "Harvey, if you can hear me, you better come out here." Not a croak came from under the couch.

I crawled on my hands and knees to the recliner chair—to the coffee table—to the TV. No frog. "Please come to Charlie," I called.

In my bedroom, I discovered—nothing!

In the bathroom—nothing!

In the kitchen . . . in the hallway . . . in my parents' room . . . in the family room—nothing!

"Look who came home with me from the shop," called my father, closing the front door.

"Grandpa! I'm so happy to see you."

"Me, too, Charlie. I see Harvey has ventured off once again."

"How did you know?"

"Because you don't usually greet me on your hands and knees. Unless, of course, Harvey is missing."

"You have a clever grandfather," said my mother, coming from the kitchen. She wiped her hands on her apron. "Since Harvey's come to live with us, Charlie spends a lot of time on his hands and knees. Charlie, take your grandfather's coat and put it in your room."

Grandpa winked as he handed me his coat. "Be patient. Harvey will be found when he's ready."

To my relief, Harvey didn't hop across the dining room during dinner. He didn't appear for mother's chocolate spice cake or to share an after-dinner cup of tea. But when Mom gently reminded me that it was time for bed, I was worried. Where was Harvey? Charles Worthington, Frog Finder, was out of patience and feeling like a failure.

I said good night, then made one more quick tour of the house. No Harvey. All during my bath, I listened for Harvey's familiar frog voice. "Where are you, Harvey?" I called. No Harvey.

In my room, I put Grandpa's coat on my chair and turned down my bed, wishing Harvey would hop out of the covers. No Harvey. I opened my closet and took out my school clothes. No Harvey. I gathered up my books and opened my backpack. Still no Harvey. One more peek under my bed.

"Charlie, may I come in?" Grandpa called from outside my door.

"Sure," I answered.

"I see you didn't find Harvey," he said.

I shook my head and stood up.

Grandpa picked up his coat. "What's this?" He reached into the pocket.

"HARVEY!"

"Rrribit!" said Harvey.

"How did he get in there?"

"Perhaps it was his favorite snack, a wilted lettuce leaf, which I always bring when I visit."

"Or maybe he misses you." I hugged Grandpa. "Thank you for finding him."

"I didn't find him," said Grandpa. "If you ask Harvey, he'll tell you he was never lost. And what isn't lost can't be found."

"Mom's right. You are clever, Grandpa."

But just in case, I put a book over the screen on top of Harvey's frog tank.

Charley's Fantastic Secret Machine

By Marilyn Marx

*H*ammer! *Hammer! Bang . . . B-A-N-G. Crash!*
"Spizzledo!"

"What's that?" Jay-Jay asked as she leaned against the kennel fence. (Jay-Jay came every day to look at Lucky's puppies. Lucky had twelve of them. There were eight left.)

"My brother, Charley, is building something," I said. "He always says . . ."

"Spizzledo!" Charley yelped.

"When things go wrong," I finished. "Come on, Jay-Jay. Let's see what he's doing."

Jay-Jay didn't move. "If I could have any pup I wanted, I'd take that one." She pointed at a fuzzy, spotted puppy who was chasing another puppy.

"You *can* have any one you want," I said, and pulled on her arm.

"My parents don't want a dog," she said.

We walked toward the shed where the sound came from. "That's the trouble," I said. "We've only found homes for four pups. We've had advertisements for free puppies in the newspaper and on the radio. We even took all of them to the school fair and brought them home again."

We reached the shed. The door was closed and locked tight.

I pounded on the door. It was so noisy that Jay-Jay helped me pound.

"Go away!" Charley yelled. "I'm building something. You can't come in."

"We want to see what it is," I said.

"No. It's a secret."

I looked at Jay-Jay, who nodded. She tiptoed around the shed while I yelled through the door. "Charley, does Mom know you're using Dad's lumber?" (My brother is thirteen and very handy. Sometimes he uses material without permission, then Dad gets mad.)

"Of course," Charley said.

Jay-Jay came back with a disappointed look on her face. "I can't see in," she whispered. "He's got the window covered with brown paper."

"I'm going to ask Mom what you're doing," I said, but Charley didn't answer. The building noises had begun again.

In the kitchen, Jay-Jay and I shared a bowl of cherries. "Mom, what's Charley building in the shed?" I asked.

"It's a secret, but if you read this, you'll know as much as I do." She gave us a clipping from the newspaper. We read:

Entries Wanted
For the Fourth of July Parade
This Year's Theme—
Real and Fantastic Machines

"That's what he's building," Mother said, "a fantastic machine for the parade. He's going to put it on the back of the truck and be a parade float. He's sent in his entry blank."

From that day on, Jay-Jay and I were more interested in the shed than the kennel. Charley never left the window uncovered or the door unlocked. Whenever we asked what the fantastic machine was going to be, he'd say, "I'm not going to tell you what it is. It's a secret. You'd blab it all over, then someone else would copy it!"

The day before the parade, the telephone rang. "It's a parade official," Mom said. "He wants to speak to Charley."

I ran to the shed and pounded on the door. "Telephone for you," I said. "It's about the parade."

Charley unlocked the door and raced toward the house. He forgot to lock the door, so I stepped inside the shed.

Before me stood a large red-and-blue contraption. Charley'd been painting white stars on it when the telephone call came.

The machine was taller than I was. I walked around it and discovered he'd used the carton the refrigerator came in for the main part. At the top, there was a cone shape that looked like a large funnel. On one side, there were steps leading up to the cone, and on the other side, a curtained opening, like a small window.

"Get out of here!" Charley hollered so loud that I took off like a Cape Canaveral rocket.

I found Jay-Jay at the kennel. There, I drew a picture of the machine in the dust. "I don't know what it is," I said.

"It really is a secret machine," Jay-Jay said. "Nobody'll know what it is."

Charley came up to the kennel. "My float will end the parade," he said. "Can you be on it?"

We nodded.

"Here's what you have to do," Charley said. "Jay-Jay, wear a long dress and this wizard's hat." He gave her a cone-shaped hat with a star on the top. "Could you make a wand?" he asked.

Jay-Jay nodded.

"You," he said to me, "are the catcher. You can wear my old Little League uniform."

I was so happy that I didn't argue.

On the Fourth of July, the signs on our float read:

THE WONDERFUL PUPPY MACHINE

Jay-Jay stood on the top step, waving her wand and pouring dog food into the cone. Inside the blue-painted refrigerator box, Charley picked up puppies and carefully threw them through the curtained window to me, the catcher. I leashed each one of them in place on the float.

Dad drove and played "How Much Is That Doggie in the Window?"* loudly on the tape deck. Lucky sat beside him, looking proud.

Kids ran alongside, yelling and cheering.

We gave away all the pups except the spotted one, which Jay-Jay is taking. Her parents finally agreed to let her have a dog.

Our float won second prize! My fantastic brother, Charley, really did build a FANTASTIC machine.

*Words and music by Bob Merrill, 1953; popularized by Patti Page.

Rosie's Summer Hummer

By Sara Lynn Kuntz

Rosie sat by the cabin's front window on a rainy summer day. Her black-and-white dog, Tennis Shoe, laid his fuzzy head on her knee. Together they watched dribbly droplets slide down the windowpane.

"What can I do?" Rosie asked. It wasn't the first time she had asked.

Her mother crossed to the screen door and propped it wide open. "Sit down over here and watch the hummingbirds. The rain doesn't bother them." She hung a bottle-shaped feeder just outside, on the eave that hung over the porch.

Rosie and Tennis Shoe settled themselves on the doormat and waited. Rosie inhaled the sweet, tangy smells of meadow grasses and sage. Tennis Shoe's nose twitched, and his eyebrows wiggled.

ZOOM! WHIZ! WHIR! Rosie saw bright green, then a silvery gray, then flashes of violet, red, and amber. The tiny birds had already discovered the fresh sugar water in the feeder. Hummingbirds darted back and forth, in and out, up and down, like daring stunt pilots determined to outdo each other with each aerial feat. Their fast-beating wings made a hum in the air.

The hummers dipped their needlelike bills into the feeder spouts. Long and narrow tongues drew quick sips of nectar. Their tongues are like built-in straws, Rosie thought.

The fairy birds hovered in midair like helicopters, and some even flew backward. One swift blur of bright green spun away from the rest. It streaked through the door, right over Rosie's head! Rosie's eyes opened wide.

"Mom!" Rosie scrambled up, stumbling over Tennis Shoe. "A hummer's inside!"

The frantic little bird zigzagged back and forth across the cabin. Rosie's heart beat as fast as the hummer's wings. Tennis Shoe barked, waving his feathery tail.

"Here's the way out!" Rosie's mother said. She waved her red-checkered apron to draw the bird back to the door. But the confused hummer rose higher and higher. It flew under and over the wide beam rafters. It shot recklessly into the loft and back out again.

The hummer's passes across the cabin grew slower. The little bird seemed tired. It hung in midair beneath the skylight, and suddenly it dropped! A spot of bright green fell to the floor. Tennis Shoe hid his eyes in his paws.

Rosie ran to scoop up the hummer. "It's smaller than my hand!" she cried. The warm bundle of feathers lay still in her palm.

Rosie's mother stroked the silky tail feathers. "Poor little thing. It's like a car that's run out of gas. It needs fuel. Let's try to feed it some sugar water."

Rosie cradled the hummer and whispered to it through her fingertips. She carefully tipped the bird back and placed the eyedropper with sugar water on its bill. A bead of nectar slid into its bill. Rosie felt a tiny jerk, like a hiccup. Another drop fell, and another. The tiny body trembled.

"Don't be afraid," Rosie whispered. Tennis Shoe's tail thumped on the wooden floor.

The hummer took another sip. Rosie smiled at the stir of feathers brushing her fingers and at the hum of awakening wings.

"Can we keep it forever? Can we put it in a beautiful cage?"

Rosie's mom touched her arm. "The bird has to spread its wings, Rosie girl. You know how miserable it feels to be closed inside, even for one rainy day."

Rosie squared her shoulders. "I'd better take him out to the porch," she said.

The screen door closed softly behind them. Rosie turned her hand and shifted the hummer to a perch on her finger. It swallowed a few more drops from the eyedropper.

"I think the bird is ready to fly," Rosie's mother said. "And look! The rain has stopped."

"Fly away, little bird," Rosie said, sweeping her hand up gently.

The hummer rose slowly and hovered close to Rosie's face. Rosie smiled, even though there was a lump in her throat. When she blinked her eyes, she was almost sure she felt the brush of a wing on her forehead, like a kiss.

A streak of bright green veered up and away, then disappeared around the side of the cabin. Rosie and her dog ran down the drying steps and into the clean-washed, welcoming meadow.

KERCHEW!

By David Lubar

"This is great," Bobby said, cuddling his new kitten. "I've always wanted a pet." He'd just returned from the animal shelter, where his parents had let him pick out a kitten for his very own.

"What are you going to name him?" his sister, Natalie, asked.

"Sherlock," Bobby said. "Just like my favorite detective." He loved to read mystery stories, especially ones about Sherlock Holmes.

"Natalie," their mother called, "something came for you in the mail."

Natalie ran down the stairs. Bobby scooped up the kitten and followed, curious to see what had come for his sister.

"It's from Aunt Sarah," Natalie said, tearing open the small package. "Oh, they're beautiful. Look, Mom." She held up one of the dozen perfumed handkerchiefs her aunt had sent her. "They're so pretty, and they smell nice, too." She tucked the handkerchief in her shirt pocket and put the box with the rest of them on the table next to the couch.

"Your aunt is so generous. You'd better write a thank-you note before you forget."

"I will, Mom." Natalie went up to her room.

Bobby put the kitten down and watched the little fuzzball run around the kitchen floor, batting at a pencil. "Thanks again, Mom. I really wanted a kitten for a long time."

"I know, and I think you're old enough now to take care of a pet."

Bobby knew he would do a good job. He sat and watched the kitten until it was time for dinner.

"Now don't feed the cat from the table," his father said as they were eating.

"I won't," Bobby said. The books he'd read about pets had warned that table scraps weren't good for animals. He petted the kitten. It purred, then jumped from his lap and went over to Natalie.

"Hi, Sherlock," she said, reaching down to stroke it. She leaned her head closer to the kitten. "He's so . . . *ah* . . . *ah* . . . *achooooo!*"

"Bless you," her parents said.

"Gesundheit," Bobby said.

"*Achoooo!*" Natalie said. She sneezed three more times, holding the handkerchief in front of her nose. "Good thing I had this," she said, tucking it back into her pocket.

"I hope you're not getting a cold," her mother said, looking concerned.

"I feel fine," Natalie told her.

The next day, the same thing happened. At dinner, Natalie had a sneezing fit after petting the cat. "Good thing I have a dozen of these," she said, putting her handkerchief back in her pocket.

"I hate to say this," her mother said, "but maybe you're allergic to the cat."

"No, she can't be," Bobby said. That would be awful. One of his friends had a brother who was allergic to cats, and they couldn't have any pets in the house except for a goldfish. He couldn't bear to even think about losing Sherlock.

Natalie shook her head. "Really, I'm fine. I . . . *achoooo!*"

The sneeze scared Sherlock from her lap. He jumped to the floor and ran from the kitchen. His soft paws made a light galloping sound as he ran toward the living room. Bobby watched him skitter away, feeling sadder and sadder. This doesn't make any sense, he thought. Natalie had been places where there were cats before. She'd never been allergic.

Just then, Sherlock came running back into the kitchen, carrying something white in his mouth. "He has one of my handkerchiefs," Natalie said.

Sherlock dropped the handkerchief, then rolled over on top of it. He sat up, then sneezed a soft cat sneeze. "That's it!" Bobby said. He ran to the living room to get the box. Coming back, he held out another handkerchief to his sister. "Here, smell this."

"I know what they smell like," Natalie said.

"Please, just smell it. Take a deep sniff," Bobby said, pushing the handkerchief in her hand.

Natalie took the handkerchief and smelled it. "I don't see *wha . . . whaaa . . . aaacchhhoooo!*"

"It's not Sherlock," Bobby said. "I took that handkerchief from the bottom of the box. It's never even been near a cat. Whenever you bent over to pet him, you put your face right next to the handkerchief in your pocket." He was so excited he picked up Sherlock and held the kitten right under his sister's nose. She didn't sneeze.

The cat sneezed again. "Maybe he's allergic to you, Natalie," Bobby joked with his sister. "That's too bad. We'll miss you." He laughed and snuggled the kitten closer.

What Can Willie Do?

By David L. Arnold

Willie was Robert and Beth's dog. They thought he was the neatest dog in the world. Beth and Robert went to daycare after school. Daycare was OK, but Willie had to stay home alone. They worried that Willie might get bored. There was not much for a dog to do all alone at home.

One Monday after school Robert and Beth talked about what they could do so Willie would not get bored.

"We can put a TV in Willie's doghouse," Beth said. "He can watch cartoons!"

"That is a great idea!" Robert said. "Where can we get a TV?"

"How about Dad's little TV?" said Beth.

They got the little TV from Dad's bedroom and took it out to Willie's doghouse. Robert crawled into the doghouse and turned on the TV.

"Find Wonder-Dog," Beth said.

"I found it," Robert called.

Beth pushed Willie into the doghouse.

"Wait!" Robert yelled. "Let me get out first!"

Willie barked at Wonder-Dog and tried to back out of his doghouse. Beth pushed Willie and Robert back into the doghouse. Willie barked louder.

"What is wrong with Willie?" called Dad.

"He is watching TV," answered Beth.

"*Bark!*" said Willie. "*Bark! Bark!*"

"Hush!" said Robert.

Dad did not think that a doghouse TV was such a good idea.

On Tuesday Robert said, "Let's teach Willie how to read."

"Dad will like that," Beth answered. "He says that books are better than television."

On Tuesday night they taught Willie how to read. Robert sat by Willie and held the books. Beth wrote the words on the chalkboard. They read *Nat the Fat Cat* and *See Spot Run*. Willie liked the stories, but he liked snack time best. He ate all the cookies.

On Wednesday morning they gave Willie some books to read while they were at school. They gave him *Nat the Fat Cat* and *See Spot Run* and a robot book. They gave him one of Dad's big car books from the bookcase because Willie liked to ride in cars.

Willie had a lot of fun with the books.

Robert found the Spot book in the doghouse. The robot book was all over the yard. Beth found Dad's car book in Willie's water dish. They never found *Nat the Fat Cat,* but then Willie did not like cats very much.

"I don't think he is very good at reading yet," said Robert.

They dried out Dad's car book and stuck the pages back in. It looked OK, almost. Then they put it back in the bookcase. They did not want Dad to get mad at Willie.

On Thursday Robert said, "We could teach Willie to draw."

"He can't hold a crayon," Beth said.

"We can teach him to finger-paint!" Robert said.

"Great idea!" Beth said. "He can finger-paint with his paws!"

Thursday night Mom and Dad went to PTA, so Beth and Robert had a sitter. Robert got out the fingerpaint and the shiny paper. Beth brought Willie to the kitchen and dressed him up in an apron. He looked neat.

They got a big bowl of water. Willie tried to drink it.

"No, no," said Beth. She put Willie's paws in the bowl of water.

They squeezed big goops of colored paint on the shiny paper. Willie had fun! He tried to eat the paint. He got paint on his paws and all over his nose. When Beth said, "Sit!" he sat in the paint.

Then they put his paws on the shiny paper, and Willie painted a very good picture. And when he wagged his tail, he painted the refrigerator!

Beth and Robert laughed and laughed. Willie barked and barked.

"What are you kids doing?" called the sitter.

"Teaching Willie to paw-paint," they said. "Come see what Willie painted."

"Oh, no!" the sitter said. "OH, NO!"

On Friday morning Mom and Dad talked to Beth and Robert.

"What are you kids doing with Willie?" asked Dad, looking confused. "First it was my TV. Then it was my car book."

"He noticed," Robert whispered to Beth.

"And last night it was fingerpaint," said Mom. "I have never seen such a mess!"

"We didn't mean to make a mess," Beth said. "We just wanted to help Willie."

"He is all alone every day," said Robert.

"We tried to teach him something to do," Beth said. "He gets bored when he's home all alone."

Dad shook his head and grinned. Mom giggled.

"Willie is a dog," Mom said. "Dogs can't read. They don't care about TV."

"Willie needs love," said Dad. "Willie needs to run and play. He will not get bored if you play with him more when you are home."

So Friday after school they got an old towel and played tug-of-war with Willie. On Saturday morning they took Willie to the park. They played tag and chase-the-squirrel and roll over. They all had a great time. On Sunday after church they cleaned Willie's doghouse, and Willie played with his rubber ball.

Beth and Robert still go to school and to day-care, and Willie still stays at home. But now Robert and Beth remember to play with Willie when they come home, and they hug him and talk to him. Willie is not bored anymore.

And Willie still likes to read.

Yesterday he ate another robot book.

A
FRIENDLY
VISIT

By Virginia Campbell Scott

Andrew Jackson was a big brown mule who lived in Kentucky many years ago. He belonged to a storekeeper, but every summer his owner would lease him and his teammate, Hickory, to the railroad.

Back in those days, before there were tractors or trucks or cars, there was a lot of work to keep a mule busy. Some days Andrew Jackson and Hickory pulled loads of crossties to help repair the track, and some days they pulled a mowing machine. But most days, Andrew Jackson and Hickory pulled a scraper. The scraper helped keep the ditches beside the railroad track clear.

Andrew Jackson's driver was a cheerful young man with curly red hair named John L. Morrison.

"Andrew Jackson, huh?" said John L. when he met the big brown mule. "Well, I think we're going to be friends, so I'll call you Andy and you can call me John L. the way my friends do."

Of course, Andrew Jackson couldn't call John L. anything because he couldn't speak, but he sure did like the talkative young man. John L. talked to the mule as they worked together. It wasn't just driver talk either, like "Giddup there, mule," or "whoa down, mule," or "Gee," or "Haw," the way other drivers talked to their mules.

John L. would say, "It's a fine hot day, don't you agree, Andy? I like it hot—and maybe I'll stop at the swimming hole after work. Doesn't that sound like just the thing?"

Andrew Jackson didn't understand most of what John L. said, but that wasn't important. He liked the sound of that friendly voice. He liked the firm, gentle feel of John L.'s hands on the reins, and he liked the careful way John L. always checked to make sure his harness fit just right and wasn't rubbing a sore spot.

Andrew Jackson liked being with John L. They were friends. Pulling the scraper didn't seem hard at all to Andrew Jackson as long as John L. talked to him.

At noon each day John L. picked a shady spot to stop for lunch. He unhitched the mules from the scraper and let the animals graze while he ate his biscuits and ham. Andrew Jackson learned to graze close to John L., because some days John L. had a carrot or an apple in his tin lunch bucket, and on those days he always shared his lunch with Andrew Jackson.

One morning John L. didn't come for Andrew Jackson and Hickory. Andrew Jackson didn't know it, but John L. had hurt his leg and was home in bed that day.

A new man came instead and drove the mules to the tracks to begin scraping. The new man was a good driver, and he seemed nice enough. But he didn't talk or sing, and he just didn't feel right to Andrew Jackson. All morning long it bothered the mule, the way it would bother a person to wear shoes a size too small.

When noon came and the new man unhitched the mules and sat down to eat his biscuits and ham, Andrew Jackson didn't lower his head and begin to graze the way Hickory did.

He had a powerful urge to find John L. The big brown mule stood, sorting out things in his memory, until all at once he remembered passing a little white house that smelled just like John L. Andrew Jackson took off, trotting to that house.

The new driver looked up from his lunch and shouted, "Hey, mule, you get back here," but Andrew Jackson just kept going, even when the man started chasing him. Andrew Jackson started to gallop, and before long he left the new driver far behind.

John L. was sitting up in his bed with his leg propped up on pillows when he heard the clopping sound of a mule's hoofs. The next thing John L. knew, Andrew Jackson stuck his head through the open window in John L.'s bedroom.

"Why, hello Andy," said John L. with delight. "Have you come to visit me?"

Andrew Jackson couldn't answer. He just stood there with a pleased look on his face.

John L. was happy to have a visitor, and it didn't matter that Andrew Jackson couldn't talk because John L. could talk enough for two.

After about twenty minutes, John L. could see that the mule was getting restless. Andrew Jackson began to shift his feet and look over his shoulder. John L. knew what was wrong.

"I reckon it's time for you to get back to work, Andy," he said. "It was mighty kind of you to come visit me, but you better get along back to the scraper."

With a last look through the window, Andrew Jackson turned around and began trotting to the railroad tracks where he had left Hickory and the new driver.

That evening John L. sent his little brother to tell Andrew Jackson's owner where the mule had been at lunchtime. The next day the storekeeper told the new driver not to worry if Andrew Jackson ran off when he unhitched the mule at noon.

"He's just making a friendly visit," the storekeeper told the new driver. "He'll be back when it's time to start back to work."

And he was.

THE GOBLIN
IN THE
PUMPKIN PATCH

By Marilyn Kratz

Usually, Kelly could hardly wait to carve a jack-o'-lantern and hang up black and orange decorations as Halloween drew near. But this year there wasn't a sign of her favorite holiday anywhere around the house.

"Tomorrow is Halloween," said Mom after school. "Don't you want a pumpkin to carve? You used to enjoy doing that."

"Nothing's fun anymore—without Lucky," said Kelly. She didn't touch the milk and cookies Mom had set before her.

43

"We all miss him," said Mom, gently smoothing Kelly's hair. "He was a great dog. But he was old and sick. All we can do now is remember the good times we had with him while he was alive."

"It's not easy," said Kelly. She took a swallow of milk to wash down the lump in her throat.

"He's been gone several weeks now," Mom went on. "Perhaps we should think of getting another dog—"

"No!" Kelly interrupted. "I don't ever want another dog."

Mom sighed. "Well, I feel we should get a pumpkin to carve into a jack-o'-lantern. Sam would enjoy it so much."

"Okay," Kelly muttered, heading for her room. "But I don't want to talk about getting another dog. There's not a dog in this world that could take Lucky's place."

Kelly's little brother, Sam, chattered happily about jack-o'-lanterns as the family drove out to the Schwartz farm after supper. Mr. Schwartz drove them to the cornfield in his pickup truck.

"The biggest pumpkins are along those tall rows of unpicked corn by the fence," said Mr. Schwartz. "You may choose any one you like."

While Sam stopped to examine every pumpkin, Kelly pulled her jacket closer around herself and made her way alone to the farthest corner of the patch. She wasn't sure whether the shiver she felt was from the cool breeze, or from the eerie stillness of the vast field in the setting sun's rosy glow. She missed Lucky's comforting presence.

Suddenly, Kelly stopped. Had she seen something white in those rows of corn beyond the pumpkin patch? Kelly looked again, but she saw nothing.

She hurried to look for a nicely shaped pumpkin. She spotted one at the edge of the patch that looked just right, and ran to it.

As Kelly knelt beside the huge pumpkin, she heard someone or something stirring in the weeds nearby. Kelly looked back toward the others. She hadn't realized that she had come so far. If only Lucky were here with her.

I must have Halloween jitters, Kelly told herself, glancing around. Although she saw nothing unusual, she couldn't shake the feeling that she was not alone.

Kelly decided to take the pumpkin she had been examining. Quickly, she snapped it from the vine and started back toward the pickup. The rows of corn beside her seemed full of shadows and rustlings. Then, right behind her, Kelly was sure she heard soft footsteps.

"Who—who's there?" Kelly could hardly gasp out the words. Slowly, she turned around. A few steps behind her was a small black-and-white dog, looking up at her with big friendly eyes.

"Kelly, what's keeping you?" called Dad, starting across the field with Mr. Schwartz.

"I'm here," Kelly called. "But I'm not alone."

"Well, here you are, you little hobo," said Mr. Schwartz to the dog as he and Dad approached. "I thought you'd gone for good when I didn't see you around all day."

"I didn't know you had a dog," said Kelly, laughing shakily. "For a while, I thought he was a Halloween goblin."

Mr. Schwartz laughed. "He's been around here for about two weeks now. I put an ad in the paper and made a few calls, but no one claimed him. I guess he's just a stray."

The little dog sat beside Kelly and lifted a paw as if he wanted to shake hands with her.

"Looks as though he wants to be friends," said Dad, smiling.

Kelly stooped to pet the dog. The little dog wagged his tail as he licked Kelly's hand. A warm feeling came over Kelly. It seemed to push out some of the cold sadness that had been inside her ever since Lucky's death.

"What are you going to do with him?" Kelly asked Mr. Schwartz.

"I'm not sure," said Mr. Schwartz. "I can't keep him here. I already have two dogs."

Kelly picked up the dog. He nestled in the girl's arms. "He needs a friend," said Kelly, almost to herself, "Just like I do."

She glanced at Dad. Dad smiled and nodded.

"How about letting us take him, Mr. Schwartz?" asked Kelly. "I think we can find him a home."

"I think you've found it already," said Mr. Schwartz.

Kelly hugged the little dog. "Come on, Goblin," she said. "Let's go home."

COWBOY KENNAN
AND THE
AWFUL WISH

By Diane Burns

Fearlessly, Cowboy Kennan twirled his make-believe lasso at the buffalo-cloud stampeding high above his tree house in the swamp.

Up, up, and gone! The pretend rope tamed the fierce beast. Hurrah for the trusty lasso that never missed its mark!

A wild cougar-cloud stalked into range. Brave Kennan-the-Cowboy roped it safely. Cowboy Kennan . . . Hero!

Now, a towering white stallion threatened. Kennan twirled his imaginary rope. He wished out loud. "Stallion-cloud, surrender. You are no match for Cowboy Kennan-the-Hero."

Kennan watched the sky, his smile twisting into a mouthful of fear. It couldn't be happening, but it was: above his head, a piece of the stallion-cloud was falling. Really falling!

"How can it fall?" wondered Hero Kennan. "I was only wishing."

Still, the white shape fell, faster and faster.

Whump! With a sickening sound it smacked into the swampy ground nearby.

Horrified, Kennan scrambled down the tree trunk and stood over the fallen prize. It was no cloud. It was no runaway stallion.

"It's a bird," he whispered.

A big white bird with outstretched wings lay stomach-down. Its bright eyes watched Kennan; its orange bill stabbed at Kennan's tennis shoes.

"Fly, Bird," Kennan pleaded. "I wished at a cloud, not at you."

But the bird could not fly. Its wings, wider than Kennan could reach with both arms, flopped weakly against the marshy earth.

The bird was hurt. And though Kennan didn't understand how, his wish was to blame. Still, no one else knew about his awful wish; no one would find the bird. Cowboy Kennan wouldn't get into trouble if he kept quiet. But what about Kennan-the-Hero?

Kennan scuffed his tennis shoe against a clump of grass. Heroes had no choice. They faced trouble head on.

"I have to get Dr. Maggie," Kennan-the-Hero decided. "She fixes animals. Stay here, Bird."

Could he get Dr. Maggie in time? Cowboy Kennan was not fast on his feet. Maybe even Hero Kennan would not move fast enough to save the bird.

"It's time for a runner," said Kennan.

So Kennan-the-Runner raced through the swamp, pounding "awful wish, awful wish" into the ground with every step. Kennan-the-Runner ran with the thudding rhythm in his ears all the way to Dr. Maggie's.

Dr. Maggie opened her clinic door. "Hello, my cowboy friend . . ."

"Come quick," Kennan gulped. "I . . . I . . . hurt a big bird with . . . my make-believe rope and a wish." How awful the truth sounded out loud!

Dr. Maggie grabbed thick gloves and a blanket. She followed Kennan-the-Runner into the swamp.

But because he was pretending to be a runner and because he was in a hurry, Kennan forgot exactly where the wild bird lay. Could he find it again before it was too late?

It was Kennan-the-Explorer who never stayed lost for long. So Explorer Kennan led Dr. Maggie past cedar trees and swamp grasses straight to the tree house. Straight to the wounded bird.

Dr. Maggie knelt. Kennan held his breath.

"It's a swan," Dr. Maggie said. She touched Kennan on the shoulder and pointed. "Do you see the bloody bruise, here under the wing?" she asked gently. "Wishes and a make-believe rope did not cause this trouble."

Hero Kennan breathed a long, relieved sigh.

With gloved hands, Dr. Maggie snuggled her blanket around the bird. She said, "You did not hurt this animal, but something, or someone else, did. We can help by taking it quickly to the clinic."

Kennan-the-Runner smiled.

"And we won't get lost?" Dr. Maggie asked with a twinkle in her eye.

Explorer Kennan said, "Of course not."

Dr. Maggie stood up, cradling the tired swan in her arms. "Kennan-the-Rescuer, you are indeed a fine friend and a hero." Then she asked, "Will Cowboy Kennan still protect us from trouble on our way home?" She smiled a gentle smile.

Kennan-the-Cowboy-Hero-Explorer-Rescuer twirled his pretend lasso at clouds overhead, and smiled back.

The Right Dog

By Jean E. Doyle

Blake saw the truck deliver the crate to Mrs. Carey's front door. He dashed over to see what his favorite neighbor was getting.

"Oh, my," Mrs. Carey said as small sounds came from inside the crate. With a hammer she carefully removed several slats. Out bounded a small bundle of white fur.

"It's a puppy!" exclaimed Blake.

"A terrier!" laughed Mrs. Carey.

The puppy leaped back and forth between them, then raced around the yard. He scampered right through the flower beds.

Mrs. Carey laughed again and said, "It's a good thing I have a fence around this yard."

She took another look at the crate and smiled, "Just as I thought. My son, Tom, sent this little whirlwind to me. He knows how much I miss my old dog."

When Blake finally caught the puppy, they gave him some cool, fresh water. But that was like putting a tankful of gas into a car, because he bounced around the yard again like someone on a pogo stick.

"I'll call him Bouncer," said Mrs. Carey.

"I'm saving up my money," Blake confided in her. "My mother says I'm now responsible enough to care for a dog if I buy it with my own money. I have almost $10 already, but it will be awhile before I have enough."

Bouncer was the perfect name for the new puppy. He never walked, just ran. He played till he collapsed, then bounced awake again a short time later.

Bouncer woke up every morning at five o'clock, ready for a new day of activity. Mrs. Carey stumbled sleepily out into the backyard with him just as the sun was coming up. Then she prepared his breakfast of Puppy Crumbles. Three times a day Mrs. Carey had to stop what she was doing to feed Bouncer again and then walk him. Actually he walked her!

After two weeks Mrs. Carey sighed and said to Bouncer, "I'm not sure Tom knew what he was giving me. I just hope you grow up soon."

A week later Blake noticed that Mrs. Carey was looking tired. He was delighted when she asked him, "Can you take Bouncer for three walks every day and play with him? I'll pay you a dollar a day."

"I'll put that money into my dog fund," he said. "Then I'll be able to get my own dog sooner." Besides, he was learning just what it takes to care for a dog.

But even with his walks with Blake, Bouncer was still a very lively dog. He loved to hide Mrs. Carey's slippers. He snatched towels and dragged them around the house. Mrs. Carey said he was the world's best hole-digger. He yapped at all the neighbors and growled at any squirrels that came near his yard.

Clearly Mrs. Carey had a problem, but giving Bouncer away was not something she wanted to do. After just four weeks she'd grown very attached to him.

In mid-July Mrs. Carey's son, Tom, came to visit her. At once he could tell that Bouncer was too much dog for his mother. He also saw that the dog was very fond of Blake and their walks.

Tom had an idea. He had a talk with his mother, and she agreed with him.

After lunch Blake brought Bouncer back from his noon walk. Tom said to his mother, "I want to take you somewhere this afternoon. Blake and Bouncer can come, too."

They all piled into Tom's van and drove to a long brick building. In the back of it they could see pens surrounded by high wire fences. Bouncer sniffed the air and began to wag his tail.

They walked in the door under a sign that said ANIMAL SHELTER.

"May I help you?" asked a pleasant woman.

Tom explained, "My mother is looking for an older dog who is calm and friendly."

The woman handed Mrs. Carey a sheet of paper and said, "Please fill out this form so that we'll know what kind of home you can provide for a dog. Then you may look at the dogs in the pens and select the one best suited to you."

The woman looked at Bouncer, who was having a hard time trying not to bounce. Blake picked him up to calm him.

"Are you trading in this little darling?" she asked. "If you do, he will be adopted before nightfall. He's just the kind of dog a lot of people want."

"Oh, no," Tom assured her. "I have already found a new home for him."

Blake's face fell. He had grown very fond of Bouncer and was beginning to feel that he and Mrs. Carey owned him together. He would miss the little whirlwind when he left.

Just then Mrs. Carey saw a gray bundle of fur with big sad eyes sitting forlornly in the back of a cage. She exclaimed, "Look at this sweetie!"

She read the sign attached to the pen: *MAUDIE—MIXED BREED—FIVE YEARS OLD—HOUSEBROKEN—SWEET TEMPERAMENT*

"This is the right dog for me," she said to Tom. "We even look a little bit alike."

While Mrs. Carey filled out the adoption papers for Maudie and paid her fee, Tom took the dog outside for a walk. Blake also walked Bouncer, who seemed overjoyed at having another dog to play with.

When Mrs. Carey came out with her papers, Blake asked, "Who is Bouncer's new owner?"

Tom smiled, "You are. I talked to your mother while you were walking Bouncer at noon. She agreed that you would be a responsible dog owner. So he's yours."

Blake gave Bouncer such a big hug the little dog grunted, then licked his new owner's face.

Blake said, "I have $23 saved up. Let me pay you for him."

"I have a better idea," Tom said. "Use that money to enroll him in a dog training class. A dog with good manners is a real joy to live with. And Bouncer is smart—he'll learn fast."

In the back seat of the van Bouncer and Maudie exchanged sloppy kisses. And Mrs. Carey was very happy that now she and Blake each had the right dog.

TIME TO MOVE ON, CAT

By Carolyn Bowman

Cat crawled out of the old wooden crate on the beach. His whiskers twitched in the cold air. Fat white snowflakes stuck to his nose and bothered his wide yellow eyes. His tail swung to and fro. "Time to move on," Cat meowed.

The pier overhead was deserted. The kindly fisherman who had shared his daily catch with Cat was now sitting in a soft, warm chair, his feet close to a blazing hearth. He had no plans to return to the pier until spring.

Sea gulls who had screamed over the ocean and sandpipers who had scooted along the sand had already found their winter shelters. The children who had played with Cat and tossed him scraps from their picnic lunches had taken their sand toys and gone home.

Cat was cold. And hungry. And lonely.

A tumbledown shed nearby looked inviting. Cat leapt through an open window. "This will be cozy," he meowed.

But several raccoons curled in a corner disagreed. "Scram!" they hissed. "We were here first."

Their flashing, sharp claws sent Cat skittering across the floor and back through the window. "Time to move on!" he meowed.

Wind howling over the waves and onto shore slapped at Cat's face. His feet sunk in wet sand as he padded toward the street.

A trash can turned on its side looked cozy. But the inside was icy cold, and a scurry of snowflakes blasted in. "I'll be a snowman in minutes," Cat meowed. It was time to move on.

A gaggle of Canada geese flew overhead. Like airplanes, their wide wings were carrying them south, to a warm place where food would be plentiful. "Honk, honk," they cried, as if to say, "Poor cat."

Grumble, grumble, grumble went Cat's stomach. A dream of fish for supper and the coarse wind finally pushed him off the beach.

He was clomping along a road when the wheels of a passing car buried him in a snow shower. "I'm moving on!" Cat meowed, and he shook himself from head to tail.

Up ahead Cat spied a garage. "Yes!" he meowed, and scurried inside.

The space was huge—a castle for a cat! A bowl of water and a plate of strange-looking lumpy food drew Cat close.

"Hey!" barked an angry dog. "That's my food!"

The hair on Cat's back stood straight up. His eyes narrowed, and he scraped his claws on the cement floor of the garage. "Time to move on!" Cat meowed. He raced outside and up the nearest tree.

"And don't come back!" barked the angry dog.

Cat stayed in the tree for a very long time. When he finally came down and started along the road, he saw a cluster of small humans building a house of snow.

"Can I stay here?" Cat meowed, and he peeked inside the igloo.

The children reached out to pet him, and Cat was glad for the affection. But the snow house fell in, and soon the children were running away.

Cat hung his head low. "Time to move on," he meowed.

There were many houses along the way. But every door was closed. Was there nowhere for Cat to come in out of the cold?

Grumble, grumble, grumble went his stomach. Shiver, shiver, shake went his long, bony tail.

Cat stopped in front of a cozy blue house with a wide front porch.

A small human was sitting on the steps. She held out her hand and said, "Here, kitty. Here, kitty, kitty."

Music to Cat's ears! As fast as his four legs could move, he plowed through the snow to the child.

The child pulled off her mittens and dusted the snow off Cat's back. "You look so lonely," she said.

Cat curled around the child's legs.

"You look so cold," she said.

Cat pushed his face against the child's knee.

"You look so hungry," she said.

Cat meowed.

"Come with me, kitty." The child opened the door to the house.

Cat followed her inside, through a long hall, and into a toasty warm room. First he shook off the cold and the snow. Then he watched the child open several doors. From one place she took a bowl. From another she took a box. She poured milk from the box into the bowl, then put it on the floor, saying, "This is for you, kitty."

"Thank you," Cat meowed, and using his busy pink tongue, he lapped up every drop of milk.

The child returned to the front door.

Cat hung his head low. "It must be time to move on," he meowed.

"This is for you." The child picked up a blanket.

Cat watched her carry it to a blazing hearth. He watched her spread the blanket on the floor and pat it.

"Come, kitty," she said. "Come and get warm."

Cat curled up on the blanket. He watched tiny flames leap in the fireplace. He felt a small hand stroke him dry. He listened to a small voice say, "Would you like to stay? Would you like to be my kitty? Would you like a name?"

Cat climbed onto the child's lap and purred with joy.

"I will call you Beastie because you are a brave little beast who came in from the cold. You will be my best friend."

Cat meowed, "Does this mean I never have to move on again?"

The child buried her face in Beastie's warm hair and answered him with a hug.

Pancakes
and
Raspberries

By Betty Bates

My Uncle Eliphalet and Aunt Hepzibah are okay. People with names straight out of the Bible have to be okay. They're kind and friendly, and neither one talks loudly. Well, not too loudly. And when you're trying to say something, they don't interrupt more than twice a minute.

Uncle Eliphalet lives on Fourth Street. Aunt Hepzibah lives on Sixth Street. And Mom and Dad and I live on Fifth Street, in between. For my birthday, Aunt Hepzibah gave me a kitten. "Now, you be sure you take good care of her, hear me?"

Uncle Eliphalet gave me a puppy. "Maybe this will teach you some responsibility, young man."

It wasn't long before the kitten turned into a speckled brown cat and the puppy became a big red mutt of a dog. Meanwhile, between feedings and brushings and paper-training and tearing my hair, I'd managed to find a minute to write their names on their dishes with my magic marker. PANCAKES was the speckled cat. Pan for short. RASPBERRIES was the big red dog. Razz for short.

Pan and Raz despised each other.

Pan stole dog food out of the dish that said RASPBERRIES, and Razz stole cat food out of the dish that said PANCAKES. Then Pan would nip Razz in the leg, and Razz would cuff Pan on the shoulder. If Razz was asleep in a patch of sunlight on the living-room floor, Pan would push her claws into his face till he bopped her with a paw. If Pan was taking a nap on my pillow, Razz would pick her up by the neck and drop her. There'd be an awful fight, with scratching and clawing, and I'd have to break it up.

I was exhausted. In fact, I was ready to give Pan and Razz back to Aunt Hepzibah and Uncle Eliphalet to teach *them* responsibility.

I had plenty of that.

Yesterday, I took Razz and Pan out in back of the house. Razz started to dig a hole under the cherry tree, while Pan hunted for mice, I climbed into my tree house to get some rest.

All of a sudden I heard Pan screech.

Something had come out from behind the cherry tree. It was black with white stripes. A skunk. Ooh boy! It looked as if that skunk was not one bit happy about Razz being near its hole. In fact, it looked as if it was about to spray Razz with that skunk stuff that makes you smell all over. Pan stood about five feet away, making an awful racket, asking for trouble. Pan trying to rescue Razz? I couldn't believe this was happening.

All of a sudden the skunk turned and streaked toward Pan. Spray came out of him like some fountain and doused her. Before she could recover, the skunk took off for its hole by the cherry tree and disappeared. Pan had rescued Razz, but she was a stinking mess.

By the time I climbed down from the tree house, Razz was licking Pan with his big old rag of a tongue, getting skunk spray all over his face.

This was too much.

The smell was nearly gone when Uncle Eliphalet and Aunt Hepzibah barged in for dinner today.

Razz and Pan were cuddling together in the spot of sunlight in the living room. Pan purred and purred, while Razz made a gurgling sound that might have been a love song.

Aunt Hepzibah and Uncle Eliphalet stared at them. They stared and stared.

Finally Aunt Hepzibah turned to me, beaming. "You've done a truly remarkable job of bringing up Pancakes," she sang out. She gave me an extradamp kiss.

Uncle Eliphalet gave me an extremely strong slap on the back. "And you've done a very fine job of raising Raspberries. Such responsibility!" he hollered.

"No problem," I said, rubbing my cheek with one hand and the back of my neck with the other.

I wished I could pin a medal on that skunk. Talk about responsibility!

Almost Pets

By Anne Schraff

Latisha looked in the pet store window. Roly-poly black-and-white puppies played with each other. One had black markings around both eyes. Latisha smiled and said, "If you were my pet I'd call you Raccoon."

In another window there were four kittens frolicking in a basket. One of the kittens was pure white. "If you were my pet, I'd call you Snowball or Marshmallow," Latisha said.

But Latisha couldn't have a puppy or a kitten for a pet. Dad was allergic to animals. There was no way there could be a dog or cat in the house.

"Maybe you'd enjoy some goldfish," Mom suggested last week.

"Nah," Latisha said. "I don't really like fish."

"You could get an ant farm, little sister," laughed Latisha's older brother, Jamal. "You could name all those little ants. "'Course they all look alike. . . .'"

Eleven-year-old Latisha didn't think that was funny. She really did want a pet, and she was sad that it didn't seem possible.

Latisha left the pet shop window and continued home from school. Her friend Mary was coming toward her, her beautiful golden retriever dog running by her side. Latisha sure would like to have a dog like that! Mary was lucky that her dad wasn't allergic to animals.

Mary waved and ran on. The dog barked in a friendly way. It just made Latisha all the sadder. She loved animals. All except fish and ants, of course.

Latisha cut through the woods on her way home. It was just a small woods, overgrown fields where houses had once stood. They had torn the houses down, and now there were trees and bushes and wild grass.

As Latisha walked, a wren flitted by. Latisha stopped and watched the bird. She was looking for a place to make a nest. Latisha liked birds a lot. Once Mom suggested they get a canary or a parakeet, but Latisha didn't want that. Bird wings were made for flying and swooping. Latisha just wouldn't have been happy to see a bird in a cage. She would have felt too sorry for it.

The wren stayed in Latisha's mind as she came out of the woods. She wished she could help the wren find a nest. Then when the fledglings were born, Latisha could watch them and sort of feel they belonged to her, too. They wouldn't be her pets. They'd be free. But they'd *almost* be her pets because she could look out for them.

The more Latisha thought about the wrens, the more excited she became. She stopped off at the library and asked the librarian, Mr. Sanchez, if he had books on wren nests.

"Why don't you build a birdhouse for the wrens?" Mr. Sanchez suggested. "We've got some good books on how to build houses just right for various wild birds."

Latisha was soon hurrying home with a book about birdhouses under her arm. On the weekend, Dad helped Latisha build a birdhouse out of plain wood with an entrance six inches from the floor. That would be just right for the fledglings to climb to.

"And we have to drill holes in the sides and bottoms for ventilation," Latisha said, reading from the book.

Finally the wren house was finished. Latisha took it into the woods and hung it from an eye screw about five feet above the ground. "Now we'll see what happens," she said to herself.

Every day, when she got home from school, Latisha checked the wren house. It was always empty. Latisha's hopes sank. It looked as if she wasn't even going to almost have a pet! Then, one Friday, as Latisha went to take a peek into the house, a wren flew at her. Latisha's heart raced. The wrens had moved in, and they didn't want to be bothered!

Latisha ran home and decided to build some more birdhouses. She built a house for swallows and one for chickadees. The last house she built was for the screech owls. She carried them all into the woods and set them in place.

At school a few weeks later, Mary asked, "You still don't have a pet, huh, Latisha? That's too bad."

Latisha grinned. "I have wrens and swallows and chickadees and even screech owls. I've named them all, even though they don't know it! I'm watching them raise their chicks. It's a lot of fun, Mary. The birds are free and happy, but I'm helping them so they're sorta mine. Almost-pets are even better than regular pets, Mary!"

"Hey," Mary said, "would you show me how to make a birdhouse? I'd like an almost-pet, too!"

"Sure thing," Latisha said. "I'll fit you in when I'm not watching Wilma Wren and Screechie!"

Snoozer and Gramps

By Anita Borgo

Gramps never ate chocolates with fillings because he never knew what was inside. He never spoke to his new neighbor, Mrs. McMoody, because he never knew what she might say. He never took his walk at different times in the afternoon because he never knew what he might see. Gramps didn't like new and surprising. He liked old and expected. That's why he didn't like it when a strange curly-tailed brown dog slept on his front porch.

"What's this?" Gramps said to himself, even though he knew perfectly well it was a dog.

"You're blocking my way." It was time for his walk, and Gramps couldn't squeeze past or jump over the dog. He might have gone out the back door, but Gramps only used the back door on Wednesday evenings when he took out the garbage. Today was Tuesday.

If Gramps couldn't get past the dog, maybe he could make the dog move. "Come," Gramps called. The dog's corkscrew tail beat against the floorboards, but he didn't come. "Sit," tried Gramps. The dog lifted his gray muzzle and snorted, but he didn't sit.

"I see the problem, Snoozer," Gramps said, naming the dog before he realized it. "You're an old dog, and you can't teach an old dog new tricks. I'll wait until you're ready to move."

For a snack, Gramps made cinnamon toast and green tea. He ate and rocked and waited for Snoozer to move. He checked his watch—an hour late already.

During his walk Gramps always stopped at the fire station. There he watched Norman, the fireman, play checkers with Mr. Snicklittle. (Norman always won.) Then he strolled to Nancy's House of Nuts and bought peanut brittle. On the way home he checked Mrs. McMoody's flower garden for spotted bugs (a little green tea sprayed on the daisies would take care of the dotted pests).

Today Gramps wouldn't watch Norman, eat peanut brittle, or check for bugs because a strange curly-tailed brown dog sprawled across the front steps.

"Oh, Snoozer," Gramps said.

Snoozer yawned and stretched (tail end high, sniffing end low). Then he rested his graying chin on Gramps's knee. Gramps scratched Snoozer's ears and fed him toast crusts. Snoozer closed his eyes and wagged his thanks.

It was late, but a late walk was better than no walk. Gramps left without his red sweater. Snoozer followed. Soon they reached the fire station.

"Hey, Gramps, you missed a great game. I beat Snicklittle five times." Norman the fireman sat alone by a checkerboard.

"Where's Mr. Snicklittle?"

"He usually leaves by now. Do you want to play?" asked Norman.

Gramps didn't know what to say.

"Looks like your dog wants to stay." Snoozer curled up at the fireman's feet.

Gramps sat opposite Norman. "He's an old dog and set in his ways. He won't leave till he's ready. I have time for a game."

Gramps won three times.

"Come back tomorrow so you can beat Snicklittle," called Norman as Gramps and Snoozer left.

Gramps reached Nancy's House of Nuts just as she was closing.

"What do we do now?" Gramps asked himself. Snoozer crossed the quiet street and sprawled on the sidewalk in front of Charlie's Chocolates. The rich smell led Gramps inside the candy store. Charlie didn't sell peanut brittle. So Gramps bought a pound of chocolates with fillings.

Before Gramps could pop a chocolate into his mouth, Snoozer wandered toward home. Gramps followed. As they passed Mrs. McMoody's yard, Snoozer plopped by the daisies. A spotted bug landed on Snoozer's nose.

"Good afternoon," said Mrs. McMoody, "you're a little late today."

"Couldn't leave without Snoozer. He's set in his ways. You know what they say about old dogs and new tricks."

Mrs. McMoody looked at her neighbor. Gramps wasn't wearing his shaggy red sweater, or munching peanut brittle, and he was talking to her for the first time in five months. "I don't believe it," she said. "You're never too old to learn."

Gramps shrugged his shoulders, offered his pleasant neighbor a chocolate, and explained how green tea would help her daisies.

Bow-Wow-Meow!

By Ellen Leroe

Papa Bonklesby told the twins he'd buy them a pet for their birthday.

"I want a kitten!" cried Billy Bonklesby.

"I want a puppy!" cried Barbie Bonklesby.

Papa Bonklesby frowned and scratched his head.

"Make up your minds, you two," he said. "You can't have both."

Billy and Barbie looked at each other, then stamped their feet at the exact same time.

"A kitten!" Billy Bonklesby shouted.

"A puppy!" Barbie Bonklesby cried.

Papa Bonklesby threw up his hands.

"It will be a surprise," he said.

"You'll find out tomorrow morning," said Mama Bonklesby.

That night in bed the Bonklesby twins each said a special prayer.

"Dear Fairy Dog Mother," Barbie Bonklesby prayed, "please make the new pet a puppy."

"Dear Fairy Cat Mother," Billy Bonklesby prayed, "please make the new pet a kitten."

The twins found a covered basket in their kitchen the next morning.

"Is it my puppy?" asked Barbie Bonklesby, clapping her hands.

"Is it my kitten?" asked Billy Bonklesby, jumping up and down.

"You'll soon see," said Papa Bonklesby.

The mystery pet beneath the blanket began to stir.

"Bow-wow-meow!" came a voice from inside the basket. "Bow-wow-meow!"

"Bow-wow-*what?*" the twins repeated in surprise.

Their new pet popped out of the basket. It had a kitten nose, a puppy's ears, a cat's whiskers, and a dog's tail. It was half-puppy, half-kitten. It didn't purr or bark, but went, "Bow-wow-meow! Bow-wow-meow!"

The Bonklesby family stared down at their pet.

Papa Bonklesby's mouth dropped open. "That's not what I ordered!"

Mama Bonklesby fainted on the spot.

Barbie Bonklesby ran to get a ball. "I'm going to play with the half-puppy side that's mine!" She threw the ball out on the front lawn. "C'mon Bow-Wow, go fetch!"

The pet half barked and purred, "Bow-wow-meow!" and raced after the ball.

"See, it's more puppy than kitten," she told Billy. "Bow-Wow is my dog!"

But their amazing pet dropped the ball and chased a bird up a tree.

"Who says it's your *dog?*" Billy said triumphantly. "Meow is more kitten. Watch this."

He put a saucer of cream beneath the tree. The pet looked down at it with twitching whiskers. Quick as a flash, it climbed down the tree and eagerly lapped up the cream.

"Good kitty," Billy said with a smug smile.

But their mixed-up pet caught sight of the mail carrier coming up the walk.

"Bow-wow-meow! Bow-wow-meow!" it half barked and purred. There was a dangerous gleam in the pet's eyes as it jumped over the hedge and attacked the leg of the mail carrier.

"Hey!" the mail carrier shouted, dropping his sack of letters. "Call off your—uh . . . uh, whatever that mangy monster is, just call it off!"

"That does it!" Papa Bonklesby roared. "I am taking that pet back tomorrow! That *thing* is not what I ordered!"

Mama Bonklesby came to, but fainted again when she saw their pet chewing on the mail carrier's trousers.

That night in bed the Bonklesby twins each said a special prayer.

The next morning the Bonklesby twins raced downstairs to find another covered basket on the kitchen floor.

"I hope it's what I prayed for!" cried Barbie Bonklesby.

"I hope it's what I prayed for!" cried Billy Bonklesby.

"I hope it's what I *paid* for!" Papa Bonklesby growled.

The mystery pet beneath the blanket began to stir and twitch.

"I'm almost afraid to look," Mama Bonklesby whispered. But then she took a deep breath and uncovered the basket.

A fluffy white bunny tied with a big pink bow hopped out.

The twins' faces fell.

"I kind of miss Bow-Wow-Meow," said Barbie Bonklesby.

"Me, too," said Billy Bonklesby. "A plain old bunny is boring."

"Well, a plain, old, boring bunny is what I ordered and a plain, old, boring bunny is what you're getting," said Papa Bonklesby.

"Give your nice new pet a carrot," suggested Mama Bonklesby.

Barbie Bonklesby offered the bunny a carrot. The bunny twitched its nose and opened its mouth.

"Polly wants a cracker," the bunny chirped. "Polly wants a cracker."

The new pet opened colorful wings from beneath its back and flew up to the ceiling. It landed on the overhead light with a squawk.

Papa Bonklesby let out a roar.

"That does it! I'm calling the pet shop and asking to have Bow-Wow-Meow back!"

The bird/bunny swooped low over their heads. "Bow-wow-meow!" it repeated in a parrot's voice. "Bow-wow-meow!"

The Bonklesby twins cheered.

Mama Bonklesby fainted on the spot.

Pretty Fred

By Debbi Miller-Gutierrez

Gary wanted a pet. Everyone he knew had some kind of pet. Billy had a German shepherd, Grant a hamster. Even Mr. Vargus, Gary's next-door neighbor, had a bird. All Gary had was his little sister, Chrissy.

Gary knew just what he wanted. There was a spotted puppy in the pet shop that wagged its tail whenever it saw Gary. "Fifty dollars and he's yours," the shop clerk, Miss Rowan, told him.

"Mother, may I have that puppy?" Gary asked his mother.

"If you earn the money," his mother said, "you may buy it."

So Gary did everything he could to earn the money. He raked leaves, washed cars, and mowed lawns. In two weeks he had almost enough. He went to the pet shop look at the puppy.

"A woman was in here asking for that puppy," Miss Rowan said. "She was very anxious to have it for her daughter's birthday tomorrow."

"But I almost have enough," Gary cried. "I only need five more dollars."

"She said she'd come back at five o'clock," said Miss Rowan, "so if you have all the money before then, you can have the puppy."

Gary ran home. He knew Mrs. Schmidt would give him five dollars to trim her ivy. But he'd have to hurry to get that huge yard done by five.

His mother stopped him as he was racing up the stairs to change into his gardening clothes. "I'm entertaining the PTA tonight, Gary, and I need you to watch Chrissy for me while I clean the house and make the refreshments."

"But I have something important to do before five o'clock," Gary said.

"I'm sorry," his mother said, "but watching Chrissy is important, too. Please go outside and keep an eye on her."

Gary went slowly down the back steps, wishing Chrissy were old enough to play by herself.

Now he would never have time to make the money he needed, and the puppy would be gone. He sat down on the steps and put his chin in his hands.

Chrissy was making castles in the sandbox and Gary could see dirt all over her face. "Are you eating dirt?" he asked her, and she nodded happily. Gary took her to the faucet and washed her face. "You don't want germs in your mouth, do you?"

Chrissy laughed and ran to chase a yellow butterfly. Gary sat down again and watched her. Chrissy was barely three, and she could move fast. Gary had to keep his eyes open.

Mr. Vargus was moving suitcases out of his garage next door. He laughed at Chrissy chasing the butterfly.

"She's a handful, isn't she, Gary?" he said.

"She sure is," Gary agreed.

Just then the butterfly flew over the wall, and Chrissy went *ker-splat* in the mud. She sat in the mud and cried.

Gary raced over to pick her up. "Poor Chrissy," he laughed. He brushed off as much mud as he could and sat her on the steps. "Stay here," he said, and went inside for a washcloth. Chrissy squirmed and cried while he washed her face.

"Once there was a little pig," Gary said, "who fell in the mud whenever he went for a walk."

Chrissy stopped crying. "Did he like to fall in the mud?"

"No," said Gary, "and he hated baths."

"Oh," said Chrissy, forgetting to squirm while Gary scrubbed her ears.

"Then one day he was walking by a pond," Gary said, "and his mother pushed him in." He cleaned Chrissy's hands. "And he was clean, just the way you are now."

Chrissy gave Gary a hug and ran to the swings. Gary pushed her way up high. Chrissy could be fun, he decided, maybe even as much fun as a puppy. Little sisters weren't all that bad.

Gary was helping Chrissy build a block tower when his mother called, "Gary, bring Chrissy in for a cookie. There's someone here to see you."

Gary sat Chrissy at the kitchen table. His mother put down a plate of chocolate chip cookies. "Mr. Vargus is at the door," she said.

Gary went to the front door. Mr. Vargus was standing on the porch, a cloth-covered square at his feet.

"Your mother and I agree that you can help me out, Gary," Mr. Vargus said.

"Me?" said Gary, his eyes on the square thing.

Mr. Vargus smiled. "I wasn't really sure until I saw how well you took care of your sister today. Then I knew you were just the one to help me." He took off the cloth, and Gary could see a big black bird in a cage. "You remember Fred," Mr. Vargus said. "Well, I'm going on a long trip next week, and I can't take him with me. Do you think you could watch him until I come back?"

Gary opened his eyes wide. Fred was a mynah bird. He could talk, and a talking bird, even for a little while, was better than any hamster, or even a spotted puppy.

"Yes, please," Gary said. "I'll take extraspecial care of him."

"I know you will," said Mr. Vargus. "Good-bye."

Gary looked at the bird. "Hi, Fred."

"Pretty Fred, pretty Fred," said the bird, putting its head to one side to look at Gary. "Fred want a cracker."

"Okay," Gary laughed, "you can have a cracker." He took Fred inside to show Chrissy.

Fritz and the Halloween Cat

By Sandra E. Guzzo

Fritz was a big fuzzy dog. Everybody in the family loved Fritz.

The mother loved him. She fed him treats when he was especially good.

The father loved him. He played fetch-the-ball with him.

The little girl stretched her arms all the way around to hug him. She said, "I love you, you big fuzzy dog."

The boy loved him, too. He laughed when Fritz

sat up and shook paws. He said, "Good dog!" and scratched him behind his big fuzzy ears.

Fritz had the best family in the whole world.

Then one day, the day after Halloween, a cat showed up. She was a fluffy, striped kitten, as orange as a pumpkin. She showed up on the front doorstep and meowed and meowed. The mother let her in!

She said, "Poor kitty. Did you get lost on Halloween?" The family called her the Halloween Cat. They petted her. They played with her. The orange cat purred and purred.

That bratty cat hissed and spat at Fritz. When he growled back, the mother, the father, the little girl, and the boy said, "No, Fritz, no!"

The mother fried fish for supper, and she gave the kitten a little piece. When Fritz sat up and begged, the mother said, "No, Fritz, no. You don't like fish."

Fritz sagged and slumped by the stove.

When the father came home, the cat didn't spit or hiss then. Oh no. The orange cat purred and purred. She climbed on the father's lap. She crawled up to his shoulder and stuck her furry little face into his shirt pocket. The father chuckled and stroked the Halloween Cat even more.

When Fritz tried to poke his nose into the shirt

pocket, the father said, "Go away, Fritz. You'll rip my pocket."

Fritz slouched in the corner.

The little girl pulled a piece of yarn in front of the cat's pink button nose and laughed when it batted the ball of yarn across the floor.

When Fritz tried to catch the ball of yarn, the little girl said, "No, Fritz, no! You'll unravel it."

Fritz left the room, his head down.

In the morning, the boy said, "You know what that little cat did? She slept on my bed and kept my feet warm."

That night, Fritz jumped on the boy's bed.

The boy said, "Get off! You're too big!"

Fritz slipped off the bed and collapsed in a large, sad heap.

Then one day, the mother said, "The Halloween Cat must belong to someone. It's too well behaved."

Fritz perked up his ears.

"I think I will call the radio," the mother said.

The next day, someone came. Fritz followed the mother to the door. There stood a big man in cowboy jeans and a checkered flannel shirt. But the man shook his head when he saw the Halloween Cat. "No, that's not my cat. My cat is much bigger and not so orange."

"Too bad," said the mother.

Fritz sagged even more.

The mother said, "I know, I will put an ad in the newspaper under 'Pets Found.'"

Two days passed, and no one came for the cat.

Fritz slouched in his corner and glowered.

The fluffy orange cat picked up its paws, one by one, and pranced closer to Fritz.

Fritz whined and put his paws over his eyes.

Bat, bat went the Halloween Cat at Fritz's nose.

Fritz peeked over his paws.

Purr, purr went the cat and rubbed against Fritz's thick, furry side.

Fritz scooted away.

The orange cat did not go away. She batted Fritz's long, silky tail.

Fritz bounded into the family room. The orange cat followed. Fritz hid behind the sofa, but the cat found him. She batted his nose, but this time she pulled her claws in.

Fritz chased the little orange cat downstairs into the work room.

The fluffy little cat leaped to the workbench and hid behind the shiny metal toolbox. Fritz barked. The cat jumped down, stood on her hind legs, and batted him on the nose again. This time . . . even more softly.

The cat twisted away and sprinted up the stairs.

Fritz chased her. Up the stairs, down the stairs, into closets, under chairs, under tables, over and under the beds.

They both skidded down the hallways. Fritz hadn't had so much fun in a long time.

When they were tired, they rested. Fritz flopped down on the living room rug. The little orange cat lay next to him and purred and purred

Then one day, the doorbell rang. The mother opened the door. A young woman with a newspaper in her hand stood there. She pointed to something she had circled.

"You have a small orange cat found on Halloween?" she asked. "I lost her that night. The trick-or-treaters spooked her. Do you have my cat?"

The mother smiled. "We may have your cat." She scooped up the Halloween Cat and showed her to the young woman.

"Oh, my Tiki," the young woman reached out and held the soft, fluffy kitten. "At last, I found you." And she took the little orange cat with her.

Fritz lifted his fuzzy ears and whined, but the cat was gone.

The mother said, "You were good to that kitten." Fritz stood tall. She gave him a Doggy Treat. Fritz knew he was special.

When the little girl came home, she hugged

him and said, "I love you, old fuzzy dog." Later, when the boy came home, Fritz held out his paw, and the boy said, "You're the smartest dog in the whole world." The father played go-fetch with him. Fritz chased and chased the ball.

Then the family wondered if they should get another kitten. Fritz lifted his ears and thumped his long, silky tail. A cat to play with would be nice. Maybe it would even be as orange as a pumpkin. Fritz had the best family in the whole world.